W9-CDU-905

Weekly Reader Children's Book Club Presents

Truman's Aunt Farm

Jama Kim Rattigan

Illustrated by G. Brian Karas

Houghton Mifflin Company
Boston 1994

This book is a presentation of Newfield Publications, Inc.
Newfield Publications offers book clubs for children from preschool through high school. For further information write to: **Newfield Publications, Inc.,** 4343 Equity Drive, Columbus,Ohio 43228.

Published by arrangement with Houghton Mifflin Company. Newfield Publications is a federally registered trademark of Newfield Publications, Inc. Weekly Reader is a federally registered trademark of Weekly Reader Corporation.

Library of Congress Cataloging-in-Publication Data

Rattigan, Jama Kim.
Truman's aunt farm/Jama Kim Rattigan; illustrated by G. Brian Karas.
p. cm.
Summary: When Truman sends away the coupon for an ant farm given as a birthday gift by his Aunt Fran, he gets more than he bargained for when aunts start showing up and he must train them all.
ISBN 0-395-65661-3
[1. Aunts—Fiction.] I. Karas, G. Brian, ill. II. Title.
III. Title: Truman's ant farm.
PZ7.R19386Tr 1994 93-4860
[E]—dc20 CIP
AC

At eleven o'clock a package arrived for Truman. It was a birthday present from Aunt Fran. Truman looked at the box. It was not moving. He gently picked it up. It felt empty. He turned it over, then smelled it. Presents from Aunt Fran had to be handled very carefully.

Truman slowly opened the box. It was empty! No, there were two cards. The yellow one said: "Happy Birthday dear Truman! I am giving you the ant farm you wanted. Love, your charming Aunt Fran."

The green one said: "Mail this card right away to receive your free ants! Watch them work! Watch them play! Watch them eat! Live ants!"

Truman mailed his card right away. Oh boy. Live ants! Live ants for his very own!

But he didn’t get ants. He got *aunts*.

It was true. There were aunts everywhere. They all loved Truman and made such a fuss!

"My, how you've grown," said Aunt Lulu.

"Isn't he handsome?" said Aunt Jodie.

"Looks just like me," said Aunt Ramona. And they hugged him, and patted his head, and pinched his cheeks, and talked his ears off.

Dear Charming Aunt Fran,

Thank you for the birthday present.
I have fifty-something aunts at my house now.
More are arriving daily. What shall I do?

Love,
Your bug-loving nephew, Truman

P.S. What should I feed the aunts?

Truman looked out his front window. A long, long line of aunts was waiting to get in. They brought their knitting and homemade banana bread and gave Truman more than one hundred-something gift subscriptions to children's magazines.

"Help!" yelled Truman.

"Letter for you," said the postman.

My dear Truman,

I am glad you liked the present. Don't let those ants bug you. Do you have any friends who would like some ants?

Love,
Your clever Aunt Fran

P.S. Feed the ants ant food.

Since they were *his* aunts he wanted them to be good aunts. What was the best aunt food? Not coffee, the aunts stayed up all night. Not alphabet soup, the aunts talked too much. Certainly not chocolate, the aunts kissed him all the time.

So Truman fed them rice pudding for breakfast, jelly sandwiches for lunch, and little hot dogs for supper.

Every morning, all the aunts lined up for inspection. Truman walked up and down the ranks. He looked over each aunt from head to toe. They were ready to get to work.

The aunts got water and sun and fresh air. They blew bubbles, flew kites, and found birds' nests. Aunt Amy could do back flips with her eyes closed.

The aunts were strong and happy. They were charming and clever. They slept, played, sang, danced, and talked just enough.

Dear clever Aunt Fran,

I have around two hundred-something aunts now. I love them all. More aunts keep coming and coming. They are the best in the world.

Love,
Your aunt-loving nephew, Truman

Yes, they were very good aunts. But they weren't really *his* aunts. And he was running out of room. Could he give them away? Who might want them?

Truman put up a sign:

Truman looked out his front window. A long, long line of boys and girls was waiting to get in.

"I want a funny aunt," said one girl, "one who knows jokes and stories."

"I want my aunt to do cartwheels," said a little boy, "and not cry if she falls down and gets dirty."

"Make mine lumpy and soft. A good cuddler," said another boy.

Truman let all the boys and girls in. They looked over the aunts from head to toe. They watched the aunts work and play. They watched the aunts eat. The aunts could tickle, tell stories, do headstands, and roller skate. When the children talked, the aunts really listened. They didn't pat heads, pinch cheeks, or talk ears off. But they still hugged.

Soon, each child found just the right aunt.

"Goodbye, dear Truman!" called the aunts.
"Thanks for a tiptop time."

Truman was sad to see the aunts go. He watched them tiptoe away. He was glad those boys and girls got their own aunts, but something was missing.

At eleven o'clock the next day another package arrived. Truman looked at the box. It was moving. He tried to pick it up. It was too heavy. He smelled it. It smelled like roses. Carefully, he opened the lid.

Out jumped Aunt Fran!

"Surprise!" She gave Truman a big hug. "But where are your ants?" she said. "I wanted to see them."

"Oh, Aunt Fran! The aunts are gone. They have their own nieces and nephews now."

Aunt Fran put her arm around Truman. He saw the twinkle in her eye. "You did a wonderful thing," said Aunt Fran. "Let's celebrate your birthday."

Truman and his very own Aunt Fran shared a special day. They had rice pudding for breakfast, jelly sandwiches for lunch, and little hot dogs for supper. They even had a tickle contest, but they were too full to do headstands.